MOUSE
and the Mystery Box

Alanna Betambeau

Illustrations by Daniel Rumsey

YouCaxton Publications
Oxford & Shrewsbury

ISBN 978-1-912419-97-5
Published by YouCaxton Publications 2019

YCBN: 01

YouCaxton Publications
enquiries@youcaxton.co.uk

Contents

Chapter 1. The Big Wide World

The bakery door closed with a click behind him and Mouse took a deep breath. He coughed and choked. The smell of the street was intense. Gone was the familiar aroma of freshly baked croissants, and Mouse's nostrils were hit by strange, strong scents. He twitched his whiskers and held a paw to his mouth as he tried to get his bearings. The road was busy with cars and motorbikes racing past, chugging out fumes. Mouse's tail flicked towards the bakery door as if urging him to turn back.

With his little heart pounding, Mouse ignored his jittering tail and unfolded the napkin that he'd tucked beneath one arm. He grasped the napkin as if his life depended on it. On one side of the napkin was a map with an arrow pointing to the doorway of his beloved bakery with the words, 'YOU ARE HERE'. Mouse felt relieved; at least the map was correct so far. It showed a library on the opposite side of the busy road and beyond the library was an area labelled 'Park'. Mouse's grandfather, who had given Mouse the map, had coloured this area green. The map showed the bustling High Street with its many shops and restaurants and a row of bus stops. His grandfather had doodled a yellow bus and had written 'The number 32 for Pierre's'.

Mouse strained his eyes in the bright sunlight and spotted the stone steps of the city library with the tall park trees towering behind. He considered his route carefully before taking two tiny, shaky steps away from the bakery door. Smack! A foot booted Mouse so hard that he flew through the air for what felt like miles before landing in a heap much further along the pavement.

Mouse opened one eye and saw the foot had a leg and a body and a head and a mouth, and the mouth let out an ear-piercing scream:

"A MOUSE!"

With that, the whole street seemed to leap into action, hard shoes running in all directions. Some missed Mouse, but some did not. He desperately tried to dodge the swinging footwear. Were they trying to kick him on purpose? With another whack, he was

rolled at speed along the ground, landing face down in a wet gutter.

Mouse lay there with his eyes closed for a minute, giving his poor aching body a few precious moments to recover. His ears were ringing and he was afraid to open his eyes. Perhaps if he wished hard enough, he'd be back inside the bakery. He wished, but nothing happened. He slowly opened one eye at a time. Thankfully, no one seemed to have noticed him in the gutter. He sighed, feeling completely deflated and breathed in a mouthful of the water that had formed in the dip of the road. He spluttered and managed to sit himself up. He couldn't believe that just crossing the pavement had been so difficult.

Mouse tilted his head to one side as water trickled out of his ear. He was wet, bruised and miserable.

"I can't do this," Mouse whispered. "I'm not ready."

Chapter 2. The Mystery Box

This was Mouse's very first experience of the outside world. He had lived in a hole in the wall of a busy bakery his whole life, with his mother, father and grandparents. The bakery was the perfect location for a family of mice, with its endless supply of fallen crumbs and tasty leftovers. For breakfast, they'd have croissant crumbs; for lunch, chunks of freshly baked baguette; and for dinner, cheese sprinkled scones. On a really good day, they'd come across the crisp flakes of an apricot tart or a sliver of a cheese and onion slice.

The abundance of readily available food had led to Mouse being a little overweight, and his expanding waistline did not go unnoticed by his grandfather.

"One day you'll make a hungry cat VERY happy with that round tummy." Mouse did not take his grandpa's comments to heart. He felt perfectly proportioned for a house-mouse. He had no reason at all to worry about cats as there were no cats inside the bakery, and until this morning, he had never dreamed of leaving home.

The reason for Mouse's uncharacteristic departure from his warm, safe mouse hole was locked inside a box, a mystery box. Just yesterday, while Mouse was busy perfecting his favourite trick of fitting an entire macaroon into his cheeks, his parents had called him to the living room. His grandpa was resting on the cotton wool sofa and had just enough energy to hand Mouse a wooden box. He smiled faintly as Mouse peered down at the letter M that had been carved into the top.

At the sight of the beautiful box, Mouse did an excited little jiggle on the spot, flicked his tail and wiggled his whiskers. He first tried to sniff at the box's contents, hoping and praying that there might be food inside, perhaps the precious remains of an apricot tart or a left over mince pie from last Christmas. Mouse's mind travelled quickly through his list of favourite delights.

With a flurry of enthusiasm, Mouse tried to reach for the latch but his grandfather raised a paw to stop him and handed him a napkin. On one side of the napkin was a beautifully drawn map and on the other a letter, written in his grandfather's curly handwriting. Mouse began to read, feeling a little disappointed that the napkin wasn't wrapped around a pastry. He read aloud so that his parents and grandmother could hear.

'Dear Mouse,

Inside this box there is a precious gift that will be yours to treasure forever. You are kind at heart, but I do worry that life has been too easy for you. You have food and shelter, and yet you have never experienced the outside world. If you don't leave this mouse hole, you might end up regretting it. I had the best time as a young mouse when I travelled around and I want the same for you. I have therefore written a list of tasks that I want you to accomplish before you can open this box.

1. Drink rain water from a puddle.

2. Make a new friend.

3. Outwit a cat.

4. Have a picnic in the park.

5. Try the Brie cheese at my favourite café (Pierre's)

6. Ride a bus.

7. Fall in love.

Your parents will keep the box safe until you've completed the tasks. Please don't give up; I promise it will be worth it.

With all my love,

Grandpa'

His excitement and interest in what was inside the mystery box faded quickly once Mouse realised he'd actually have to work for it. Mouse was not used to hard work, or any work for that matter. He tried to hide his intrigue completely and shuffled back to his bedroom to find his macaroon.

Mouse showed no signs of backing down until his mother appeared in his bedroom doorway later that afternoon. She bore the devastating news that Mouse's grandfather had just taken his final breath. The lump in Mouse's throat grew bigger and bigger and tears rushed from his eyes. He wiped his cheeks with his tail and snuggled into his mother's warm chest.

When the shock had subsided, Mouse's mind wandered once more to the mystery box. Perhaps his wonderful grandpa had known that his time was soon to be up and this box was his parting gift. Every inch of Mouse, from his large round ears to the very tip of his tail, told him NOT to leave the mouse hole, but there was one tiny niggling feeling right at the very back of his head, like an itch that he couldn't quite reach to scratch. That niggle was his grandfather, wishing and hoping that Mouse would achieve something for the first time in his life, besides, of course, his critically acclaimed macaroon triumphs.

Mouse eventually and reluctantly agreed to his grandfather's quest, with considerable persuasion from his grandmother. She truly believed that Mouse would succeed. He felt torn between the desire to make her proud and the looming dread of letting everyone down, or worse, being killed by a cat! She confidently helped him pack his slippers, toothbrush and comb while his unsettled stomach churned.

Mouse had no idea what to expect from the outside world. It was hard to picture something he had never seen before. His mother had been born in the bakery and his father had grown up in an Italian pizza restaurant just three doors down the street. Only his grandparents had truly experienced the big wide world. Grandpa had told him countless stories about his adventurous life travelling on the London Underground. He spoke fondly of his experiences, unless of course they involved a cat. He told Mouse that cats have whiskers like cheese wire, claws like daggers and their breath smells like rotten fish. He also told Mouse that cats have brains the size of tadpoles, and that a mouse could always outwit a cat as long as there was time to think. Mouse wondered if he should have listened a little closer to his grandfather's cat escape stories. Suddenly, they had a lot more relevance than before.

After a restless night of tossing and turning, Mouse bid a sad farewell to his parents and grandmother.

"Good luck," sobbed his mother, stifling a cry, and she squeezed him so tightly that he let out a squeak. Her voice was shaking as she fought to control her emotions. Mouse headed out of the bakery feeling sick with nerves, the mystery box remaining safely in the mouse hole, unopened.

Chapter 3. A New Friend

That fearful, sickly feeling had returned, as Mouse now sat in the gutter rubbing his scuffed elbows and knees. He swivelled his head to see if he could still see the bakery door; perhaps giving up was the best option for him now. Then suddenly, Mouse realised he'd already completed one of the tasks, even if by accident. He'd drunk rain water from a puddle! This particular puddle was probably more dirt than rain, but he was willing to count that. He peered down at the pool of water and saw a mucky reflection. He had a black eye, was sure he was missing a whisker and was almost unrecognisable.

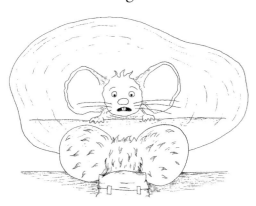

Surprisingly, his disappointed expression changed to a look of grim determination, a new look for Mouse. He'd never been determined to do anything before! He smiled at his reflection and with one task done, he clambered to his feet. He checked his scrunched map and headed in the direction of the bus stops, limping slightly and thinking of his brave grandpa as he went.

As Mouse hobbled along the gutter, he thought of his mystery box back home and considered what could possibly be inside. He felt a pang of intrigue again and his round tummy rumbled. His new guess was that it might be a cheese knife. His grandfather liked to use a knife for slicing special cheeses and said that it was good manners to do so. Perhaps this was his gift to Mouse.

He was dreaming of cheese, when he saw in front of him what he guessed might be a bus. It was a bright yellow rectangle on wheels and there were people climbing on and off it, like his grandfather had described. He sped up slightly and scurried towards a bus that had just pulled over, but without warning it suddenly spat out a thick, dark cloud from its

exhaust and sped off. Mouse sneezed, rubbed
his eyes and peered down. His beautiful soft
fur was now absolutely filthy. Falling in love
was definitely out of the question, he thought
to himself, at least while he looked like this! He

considered reaching for his comb, but decided he was probably fighting a losing battle.

He clambered back up on to the pavement wondering if he could walk to Pierre's instead. Feeling hopeful, he retrieved a couple of crumbs from his bag and stuffed them into his cheeks for energy. Thankfully, he didn't need to stumble for long. Soon after his snack stop, a second number 32 bus screeched to a halt just a little distance in front of him. He crept closer, keeping his body low to the ground, dashing between feet and trolleys, trying to stay unnoticed. He hid behind a lady's bag as she waited in the queue for the bus.

Each person in the queue stepped on to the bus, mumbled something to the driver and handed him some money, as Mouse had seen the customers do in the bakery. Mouse crept even closer, his large, pink ears stretched open as wide as they would go.

As he listened intently, he heard the woman ask, "Do you stop by Pierre's?"

The driver nodded. Without hesitation, which was very unlike Mouse, he clambered into the purple flowery bag and was lifted onto the bus. He was plunged into immediate darkness and landed on top of the bag's contents.

The elderly lady swung the bag by her side as she wobbled down the aisle to find somewhere to sit. As she slumped down onto the leather seat, the bus engine roared and a heavy object fell onto Mouse's tail.

"Ouch!" he shouted, his tail pinned down.

"Are you okay?" a small voice called out. Mouse froze, partly with fear, but mainly because the object was preventing him from moving. He waited, not even blinking, wondering where the voice had come from. He hoped and prayed that it didn't belong to a cat as he was feeling far too battered and bruised for that encounter! He sniffed for fishy breath, but could only smell cookies and the peanut butter sandwiches that were wrapped up inside the bag. He heard a rustling and a shuffling and the voice spoke again. "Are you hurt?"

Mouse's eyes adjusted to the darkness and he could just about make out the shape of the speaker. Mouse could tell that the creature was much smaller than he was, which was a relief.

"My tail is stuck," Mouse whispered back, his eyes straining in the little light that was peeking in through the bag's stitching.

"No problem," said the chirpy voice and the creature started rustling again, but much louder. Mouse felt the creature's little hands wrap round his tail and tug. Thankfully, his tail was freed. The creature that had helped him was panting.

The bus bumped over a hole in the road and the movement caused the top of the bag to open wider so that a bright beam of daylight shone inside. The little creature was illuminated before him. Mouse saw that it was small, round and was red with black dots and it didn't have a tail.

Mouse asked what kind of creature it was and it replied, "I'm a ladybird and my name is Arthur."

Arthur leapt into conversation immediately. He quickly explained that he'd been innocently nibbling the pages of a note book, when it was packed into the bag with him still on it. One of his little wings had been squashed in the fold of the book. He'd been in the bag for two days and had been desperately trying to climb or fly out, but was just too exhausted. Luckily, he had cookie crumbs and the note book to keep his hunger at bay. Mouse thought Arthur was particularly upbeat considering he'd been trapped in almost darkness for two days.

Mouse felt at ease in Arthur's company and once Arthur had finished chattering, Mouse shared his own story. He told Arthur about the list he had to complete before opening his grandfather's mystery box, and that this was his very first trip away from home.

Arthur had his own ideas of what might be inside the wooden box. Most of the ideas involved strawberry jam, which was his favourite food. His most imaginative suggestion was a magic cheese that when you ate it, you became invisible. They laughed at what they'd use their invisibility for, which included breaking into a strawberry jam factory and pulling a cat's whiskers. Mouse had never laughed so hard and Arthur was a wonderful distraction from missing his family.

Mouse promised Arthur that once the lady was safely in Pierre's, he'd be making a run for it and he would help Arthur out of the bag at the same time. Arthur was very grateful and thanked Mouse. Then he asked if he could accompany Mouse on his quest, to which Mouse agreed happily, welcoming the company. They chatted animatedly until the bus reached their stop and the lady rose to her feet.

Chapter 4. The Best Brie Ever

Mouse held on tight to the notebook as the lady bumped the bag off the bus. She thanked the driver politely and Mouse heard the sound of her clip clop shoes step off the bus and on to the pavement.

"Are you ready?" Mouse asked Arthur, who was holding on to Mouse's tail.

"Ready," Arthur replied, with a little thumbs up.

Mouse paused, hardly breathing, listening for the right moment. He heard the voices of people walking up and down the High Street, the creak of a door opening and a roar of chatter.

Arthur peered through a tiny gap in the seam of the bag and whispered, "We're in Pierre's." Mouse waited until he felt the bag being lowered to the floor as the lady took a seat at a table in the café.

"Let's go!" Mouse shouted and, with an almighty effort, he leapt toward the opening at the top of the bag and forced his way out of it. Arthur clung to his tail as Mouse skidded onto the cold, tiled floor.

They remained hidden behind the bag, giving themselves the opportunity to catch their breath. Mouse had a pain in his side from being kicked earlier, but besides the discomfort, he also felt something strange, something new. He felt excited! He wondered if this was why Grandpa spoke so fondly of the outside world. So far, his morning really had been the most eventful of his life!

Looking around the café, it was no larger than the bakery back home. The smells were similar too. It felt warm and familiar and comforted Mouse. He could hear the sounds of crockery clinking, customers chatting and the whoosh of the coffee machine. Mouse started scooping up crumbs that had fallen under the lady's table. He went to stuff them into his cheeks, but paused and politely handed the first crumb to Arthur.

"Thank you, friend," said Arthur, gratefully tucking in.

Mouse smiled. He hadn't noticed that he was now three tasks down. He'd drunk rain water from a puddle, he'd ridden on the bus and now he'd made a friend. He imagined Grandpa's look of surprise at seeing Mouse out of his mouse hole, sitting in Pierre's with a ladybird companion.

As Mouse sat thinking, Arthur started chuckling. Mouse asked him what was funny and he pointed to Mouse's foot. Mouse was sitting in a dollop of chocolate sauce and his foot was absolutely covered. Mouse laughed too and then he wondered if it would be poor manners to lick the chocolate from between his toes. He waited until Arthur had turned away, then took a sneaky lick. It was absolutely delicious! He could see why his grandfather loved Pierre's so much. Perhaps his grandfather had put the secret recipe for Pierre's chocolate sauce inside the mystery box. He day-dreamed, drooling slightly.

After savouring the safety and nibbles beneath the table, they discussed their plan for tasting the Brie cheese. Arthur suggested that he could fly up to have a look round to see if he could spot any. Arthur's plan was bold and brave and Mouse couldn't believe that Arthur would risk being swatted or squashed just for him. Mouse tried to think of a better option, but couldn't. Mouse was too big to look himself; he was sure to be noticed.

Mouse wished Arthur luck as he took flight, his damaged wing flapping much more slowly than the other so it was hard not to fly in circles. All Mouse could do was wait, anxiously counting each second that passed. Arthur fluttered his tiny wings and hovered above the table where the lady was sitting. He looked over at each of the other tables to see what the customers were eating.

He spotted a chocolate brownie, a jacket potato and a scone with strawberry jam. His

mouth watered and he had to prise his gaze
away from the jam to search for Brie.

Arthur continued to hover, getting
breathless, until he finally saw a waitress place
a bacon and Brie baguette in front of a grey-
haired gentleman. His heart gave a little jump

and he sped back down to Mouse who had
just reached 32 seconds. Mouse was so relieved
to see him unharmed that he gave him an
affectionate squeeze. Arthur was considerably
smaller than Mouse and the hug didn't quite
work, but the intention was clear.

"Table 5," gasped Arthur, looking extremely pleased with himself. Table 5 was on the opposite side of the café from the table that they were currently crouched beneath. Mouse thought for a moment before pulling his napkin out of his bag. He offered his tail once more and the ladybird clambered on. Then he placed the napkin on top of his back and ran, excitement and adrenaline rushing through his body. He ran straight towards Table 5 where the man was already tucking into his bacon and Brie baguette. A little girl pointed at the napkin moving on its own, but her mother dismissed her and, before she could shout again, they had reached the table and were safely underneath it. Mouse threw off the napkin and Arthur gave an elated whoop!

They didn't need to wait long before the man accidentally dropped the end of his baguette on to his lap and it rolled onto the floor.

"Bother," said the man. Mouse and Arthur leapt at the chunk of bread. Mouse scooped some of the Brie from the inside and first handed a ladybird sized piece to Arthur and then placed a much larger chunk into his own mouth. His mouth exploded with flavour as the warm Brie melted on his tongue. It was by far the best cheese he had ever tasted. It warmed his throat as he swallowed, leaving a deliciously delicate aftertaste. Mouse smiled at Arthur who was enjoying his piece so much that his eyes were slightly closed.

"The best Brie ever," mumbled Mouse in a daze, licking his lips.

Chapter 5. Moon Cheese

Mouse and Arthur hid beneath Table 5 for the rest of the afternoon. They chatted merrily enjoying the wealth of crumbs that tumbled off customers' knees. They lapped up cakes and treats, whilst discarding salad leaves with a grimace. Once full to bursting, they curled up together, like life-long friends, and slept.

They were woken hours later by the sound of a broom swooshing across the café floor. The café was empty of customers and the staff were clearing up ready to close. Mouse peered up at the café windows from beneath the table and saw that the sunlight had completely faded. The blue sky had been replaced with black, and street lights were illuminating the High Street.

"We need to go. Now!" shouted Arthur, closely watching the broom which had only two tables left before it reached them. Besides the immediate danger of being whacked by a broom, the door to the café would not stay ajar for much longer. Any minute now the

OPEN sign would be switched to CLOSED and the front door locked.

They watched and waited until the man controlling the broom was distracted by a sticky blob of melted cheese that was refusing to budge from the tiled floor. Mouse grabbed the napkin, threw it on top of them and they dashed out of the door onto the cold pavement.

"Where next Mouse?" asked Arthur, but Mouse wasn't listening. His head was tipped backwards and his eyes fixed on the sky.

"What are those?" he gasped, transfixed, and he raised a paw and pointed to the stars high up in the sky.

"Stars," replied Arthur. Their name was irrelevant really; all Mouse wanted to know was how he could get closer. He spun around and spotted a drainpipe that ran up the front of Pierre's.

"C'mon," he said still in a dreamy voice and he beckoned Arthur to follow him. He clambered up the drainpipe, that new feeling of determination flooding all over his body.

He scrambled up the drainpipe until he could reach across and clamber onto the striped canopy that hung above the café. He plonked himself down and sighed; the view was absolutely breathtaking. He lay back and stared up at the twinkling stars.

Arthur smiled. He had forgotten just how beautiful the stars were and he joined his friend on the canopy and told him all about star constellations and the solar system. Arthur was incredibly knowledgeable. Mouse felt embarrassed by his lack of knowledge about anything besides his mouse hole. His macaroon accomplishments were starting to feel rather insignificant in the big wide world.

As they gazed, the clouds parted and a beautiful beaming moon revealed itself. Mouse's mouth hung open. Arthur watched him contentedly.

"Some say its made of cheese," Arthur whispered with a wink. Mouse's eyes grew even wider at the thought of it. He imagined the sweet taste of moon cheese and giggled. The moon disappeared again a few moments later as thick clouds drew back in. Mouse groaned with disappointment, hoping for an encore.

"It's going to rain," said Arthur looking worried. Mouse had never seen rain before so he was excited for yet another new experience. Arthur, however, was not. "Rain drops can be as big as me!" squeaked the little ladybird. Mouse promised to protect him and tried to think, fast.

"Quick, let's check the list again," suggested Mouse, holding the napkin up towards the street lamp.

"Drink rain water from a puddle - check," and he drew a tick in the air. "Make a friend." He looked at Arthur, feeling slightly nervous.

Mouse had already ticked this task off the list in his mind, but he was embarrassed to say it out loud. Arthur wasn't embarrassed and he proudly said, "Check!" Mouse smiled and drew another imaginary tick.

There was a definite change in Mouse. He was eager and confident as he considered each task carefully. They checked off number 6 - ride a bus, and then looked at number 4. Although a picnic in the park sounded fairly easy, it didn't sound like something they could do in the rain or the dark and they'd eaten so much food in Pierre's that they wouldn't be hungry any time soon.

"Where do you live, Arthur?" Mouse asked, hoping they could spend the night there before attempting the rest of his list tomorrow.

"Wherever I fancy," Arthur replied. "I left home three weeks ago. It was a bit cramped with all my brothers and sisters".

"How many do you have?" Mouse asked. Arthur paused for a moment looking thoughtful and doing a quick count up in his head.

"56 brothers and 38 sisters, at the last count."

Mouse burst out laughing, assuming Arthur must be joking, but he wasn't. Arthur laughed too. They chortled at the idea of Mouse having that many brothers and sisters all crammed into his mouse hole in the bakery. Mouse had always been happy as an only child. He didn't have to share his cotton wool bed or his apricot tart. But hearing about Arthur's family made him realise that perhaps sharing wouldn't have been so bad after all. At least he'd have had company.

Arthur interrupted Mouse's thoughts with an unwelcome suggestion, "We could sleep in the park and then we'd be there ready for the picnic tomorrow." Mouse did not like the sound of sleeping outside in a park. The dark clouds had completely engulfed the magical moon and all of the bright stars now. The wind was picking up, flattening Mouse's fur as it blew. Mouse was beginning to feel uneasy. He wondered if they could sleep inside Pierre's, but Arthur warned him of what the owners might do if they found a mouse in their café. With no other suggestions, Mouse agreed and they shimmied back down the drainpipe and onto the street.

Mouse pictured the map in his mind, having tucked it away in his bag to keep it safe from the rain, and headed for the bus stop. Arthur was perched on top of Mouse's backpack, hiding beneath one of the straps in anticipation of the rain. They looked an extraordinary pair.

Mouse had to dodge only a few passing feet as the dark helped him to stay unnoticed. They waited for the number 32 for eighteen long, cold minutes, but only the number 20 whizzed past in the opposite direction. The rain started to fall and pitter-pattered onto Mouse's head and back. It was gentle at first then it was cold and hard. Mouse could see why Arthur didn't like it much. They sheltered under the bench in the bus stop, huddled together, urging the number 32 to hurry up. It eventually dawned on the pair that the number 32 bus was not coming.

"We'll have to walk," said Mouse, trying to sound confident in his suggestion, but quietly wishing Arthur would object. They scurried to the gutter where Mouse had crept along earlier that day, but it was flooded. The rain water was whooshing and whirling along it and disappearing down drains. It looked far too dangerous to walk.

A small cardboard box, similar in size to those that the bakery used for takeaway pastries, suddenly came rushing down the gutter stream. Arthur saw the idea ping into Mouse's mind and his eyes light up like a fire fly. He grabbed hold of the backpack in preparation. Mouse reached out a paw and grasped the box. He was able to hold it still long enough to throw open the lid and leap inside. Arthur screamed as the cardboard box, with them inside, shot along the gutter at high speed.

Arthur's screams quickly became squeals of enjoyment.

"WAHOO!" he shouted as the box tossed and turned them on the rolling waves. The box travelled all along the gutter until eventually Mouse spotted the very top of the city library roof. He held his nerve and waited for the best possible moment. With all his might, Mouse leapt out of the box and onto the pavement.

"We did it!" Mouse cheered, dancing around on the spot. Arthur threw his tiny arms in the air like a Mexican wave. The grand, ornate steps of the entrance to the library were just a few metres in front of them, with the soaring trees of the park peeking over.

Chapter 6. The Big Grey Cat

Next to the entrance sign to the park, there was a park map which showed a children's playground, a fountain, a pond and a woodland area. The rain drops splashed onto the map.

"We'll be the most sheltered in the woodland," said Arthur. Mouse was not convinced. He longed for his warm bed and for his parents to tuck him in. The cold rain seemed to have soaked through his fur all the way to his bones. His teeth chattered in the cold.

They hurried past the playground which was ghostly in the dark. It was empty of children and yet the swings and the roundabout moved on their own in the wind making a creaking sound. Mouse hummed quietly to distract himself from the eeriness. The trees were casting shadows on the pathway in front of them. Mouse hummed louder.

When they reached the fountain and large pond, Mouse stopped humming. He crept silently passed the flock of ducks that were sleeping around the edge of the pond. He held his breath trying not to make a sound, no idea of what a duck might do to a mouse who was out without his parents. Arthur was about to explain to his friend that ducks were more partial to bread than mice when he spotted something.

"There!" shouted Arthur in Mouse's ear, making him jump in the air. Luckily the ducks didn't stir.

"What is it?" Mouse asked, his heart pounding.

"A cat!" Arthur pointed over to the fountain where, sure enough, a large, grey cat was drinking from the cool water.

The cat looked enormous. Mouse thought of all the Brie he'd eaten and was seriously doubting his ability to outrun the cat. He would definitely need to outwit it, but his brain felt slow too. It really had been an exhausting day!

"You need to finish your list so you can find out what's in the box. Here's your chance to check another one off." Arthur was smiling as he spoke, as if Mouse should be grateful for his discovery of this menacing beast.

Mouse tried to remember what his grandfather had told him: "You can outwit a cat if you are clever enough because cats have brains the size of tadpoles."

Spurred on by his grandpa's words of wisdom, Mouse tiptoed closer towards the fountain and once he was about a metre away he squeaked loudly to get the cat's attention. He was ready to run and Arthur was poised to distract, but nothing. The cat continued to drink. Mouse squeaked again and the cat's ears pricked up, but it did not turn.

With a burst of bravery, Mouse shouted,

"Hey cat, you can't catch me!" The cat d e f i n i t e l y heard that time and it stood up straight and turned on the spot. It looked even bigger now that it wasn't stooped over. Mouse froze. His head said run but his feet were stuck to the ground like glue. The cat jumped down from the fountain wall, its yellow eyes fixed on Mouse.

The cat was so close to Mouse now that he could smell its fishy breath. It was not pleasant and Mouse scrunched up his nose. He was surprised that his nose had moved, as he had been completely frozen with fear. He tried to move one of his paws and he just about managed it. He tried to move his tail and it wriggled slightly. He used all of his strength to pick up one foot and, as it came unstuck, he turned to run.

Mouse had been moving in slow motion and the quick cat was ready long before Mouse was. It pressed its paw hard on Mouse's tail preventing him from escaping. Mouse strained to wriggle free, but the cat's weight was too much. Mouse's heart was beating so fast and loud it could almost be heard. The cat, on the other hand, was as calm as could be, as if catching mice was a relaxing sport.

The cat licked its lips as Mouse wondered where Arthur was with his distraction. Perhaps Arthur was frozen with fear too.

The cat leaned forward and, out of nowhere, Mouse shouted, "Wait!" as loud as he could. The cat paused, its mouth hanging slightly open. "You can't eat me..." Mouse continued. He searched his brain for an idea and a reason that might convince  the cat not to eat him. "I can get you fish, lots of fish, piles of fish," Mouse said quickly and the cat's mouth closed, luckily not around Mouse.

"What kind of fish?" the cat asked curiously, the pressure on Mouse's tail easing slightly.

"Er... salmon and cod," Mouse replied. He couldn't think of any others. He could have listed a hundred different cheeses, but fish was not his forte. He felt his nose twitch involuntarily as he lied and hoped the cat wouldn't notice.

"What about tuna?" asked the cat curiously, apparently falling for Mouse's ploy. Mouse nodded rapidly and assured the cat that there would definitely be tuna. He used his outstretched, trembling arms to indicate the size of the imaginary tuna. The cat licked its lips again and released Mouse's tail completely.

Mouse kept one eye on the cat and the other searched for Arthur who was yet to appear. Mouse finally spotted him stuck in a piece of chewing gum that had been dropped on the path. Arthur's little arms were waving frantically as he tried to free himself. Mouse couldn't hear him, but he was sure he was shouting.

Mouse could see the woodland section of the park beyond where Arthur was struggling. He wondered if he would be able to make it as far as the trees if he made a run for it, grabbing Arthur on the way. He would need a good head start as the cat's legs were much longer than his own.

"So where is this fish then?" the cat asked quite impatiently.

"How do I know you're not going to eat me as soon as I've told you?" Mouse replied, trying to stall the cat for as long as he could. The cat agreed not to eat Mouse in return for him revealing where the piles of fish were stored. Mouse was not entirely convinced that the cat would be true to his word and not eat him; he was sure the cat had crossed its paws when it gave the promise.

"It's all kept in the fish shop on the High Street and I have the key. Well, I buried the key, actually, just over there below that circle of flowers." Mouse pointed over to a ring of dandelions and the cat turned to look. Mouse's nose twitched again. "Grandpa was right," he thought, "cats do have brains the size of tadpoles!"

"Wait here," said the cat and it bounced eagerly over to the dandelions.

Mouse waited until the cat had started digging up the soil and then turned on his heels. He released Arthur from the chewing gum with a great tug and ran as fast as his legs would carry him. He felt the Brie in his tummy churning up inside and a stabbing pain from a stitch, but he didn't slow down.

He charged towards the woodland, too afraid to look back to see if the cat had noticed him.

"He's chasing us!" shrieked Arthur, clinging on to Mouse's bag. Mouse threw a quick glance over one shoulder and saw the cat racing after them looking angry and hungry.

"Liar!" shouted the cat as it bounded after them. Mouse darted from left to right and leapt over the puddles, trying desperately to outmanoeuvre the cat. Luckily, the rain appeared to be slowing the cat down slightly as it stopped mid-run to flick away the drips from its whiskers. Mouse had just about managed to stay ahead when, out of the trees, flew an enormous creature with outstretched wings.

"OWL!" screamed Arthur pointing up at the sky. The owl swooped and dived towards Mouse, its sharp talons at the ready. It's yellow eyes gleamed in the dark like two terrifying balls of fire. Mouse screeched to a halt and turned to run back, but the grey cat had caught up with them. He was starting to favour being caught by the cat as the owl seemed even more frightening and, he imagined, less easy to outwit.

Thankfully, the grey cat was not about to let Mouse be plucked from its reach at the very

last moment and leapt to protect its prize. Spitting and hissing, it swiped at the owl with razor sharp claws sending feathers flying. One of the owl's talons sliced a deep gash in the cat's back and it wailed in pain. Mouse and Arthur watched in horror before realising they were missing their opportunity to escape.

Arthur spotted a small opening in the trunk of a great oak tree. The hole looked just big enough for Mouse, but too small for the cat or the owl. He tugged at Mouse's bag and swerved him around. Mouse jumped into action and sprinted as fast as he could. He

took a head first dive into the hole, landing inside the hollow tree trunk in a heap. They pinned themselves against the back wall of the trunk and waited for the grappling pair to notice.

The owl was the first to see that their dinner had disappeared and with a loud hoot, it flew back into the trees, nursing several tender cat scratches. The cat hissed again and dashed out of sight.

"Outwit a cat - check! Do we get extra points for outwitting an owl?" laughed Arthur, suddenly feeling confident. Mouse was not ready to laugh yet or acknowledge that they'd completed another task. He could hardly breathe as his stitch had him doubled over and his heart was about to leap out of his chest.

Eventually, he felt calm enough to slide down on to his side. He curled up, completely drained and drenched from the rain, feeling very homesick. Arthur fluttered his wings to get dry and tucked himself under one of Mouse's ears, which made a perfect ladybird duvet cover. It took Mouse forever to get to sleep. Between Arthur's snores and the scary sounds of the night echoing through the trees, it was a wonder he got any sleep at all that night.

Chapter 7. Tea and Scones

Despite the poor night's sleep, when Mouse woke the next morning he felt surprisingly positive. He'd survived his first day after all. Perhaps he was more capable of coping in the outside world than he'd first thought. He gave a stretch and a yawn and enjoyed the feeling as a beam of sunlight shone in through the hole in the tree trunk and warmed his fur. Arthur crawled out from underneath Mouse's ear and rubbed his sleepy eyes.

"Picnic in the park?" he asked. Mouse checked his bag for crumbs, but everything was wet. He laughed at the sight of his slippers, toothbrush and comb. Arthur was not perturbed and had an idea. He crept quietly to the entrance of the tree, wary that the cat might still be waiting for them, then beckoned Mouse to follow.

"All clear," he said, to Mouse's great relief. The sun was shining and the park was full of life. Mouse could hear children laughing and playing in the playground. He could see mums with push chairs walking and chatting, and runners jogging and dodging the last few puddles.

Luckily, they were all too busy enjoying the park to notice a mouse and a ladybird sneaking out of an oak tree. Arthur led his friend to a patch of grass where the sun was shining down through a gap in the trees above. Mouse's fur dried in minutes; the warmth felt incredible. He rolled on his back, savouring this beautiful morning. It felt so far away from his dark little mouse hole. Mouse wondered if perhaps he might be able to put in a window when he returned home. He was really enjoying seeing the sky and the beaming sunshine. It was almost as spectacular as the night sky.

"Tea?" asked Arthur, taking Mouse by surprise. "Here you are," he said and he poured what appeared to be an invisible cup of tea and passed it to Mouse. He then poured his own imaginary cup and took a sip, followed by a long sigh, "Ahhhhh." Arthur pretended to dunk something into his tea before stuffing air into his cheeks.

Mouse didn't really know what to do. He guessed this must be a game, but with no brothers or sisters, he didn't really know how to play.

"Do you prefer jam first or cream?" asked Arthur, giving Mouse a wide smile. Mouse shrugged. "Well I always have cream on my scone first and then a big dollop of strawberry jam on top, so I'll do yours like that too." Arthur continued, pretending to spread cream and jam on to an invisible scone. He passed one to Mouse and then ate his own mouthful of air, rubbing his tummy. He made a funny "hmmm" noise. Mouse shyly nibbled his air too, not sure if he was playing the game correctly. He tried to imagine that he was enjoying the sweet taste of an apricot tart.

Mouse soon got the gist of the game and they played for a long while. At one point they were both laughing so loudly that they woke a robin who was trying to sleep in the tree above them.

"Please quieten down," called the robin from up in the tree. "I'm trying to take a nap," she said yawning. Mouse apologised and they tried to keep the noise down, but it was difficult when they were having so much fun.

They tried to play in whispers, but had little success. Arthur started a pretend food fight and Mouse hit him hard with an imaginary grape. Arthur was very theatrical and he rolled on the ground as if the grape had knocked him off his feet. Mouse could not control his laughter and he woke the bird again.

"Humph", said the bird loudly and she flew down from her branch and landed on the grass by Mouse and Arthur. As she landed, she angrily fluffed her feathers. The bird had brown wings and a beautiful red breast.

"Now, I normally wouldn't mind, but today I need my sleep," explained the bird, glaring at Mouse and yawning again. The robin, who introduced herself as Rosie, told Mouse and

Arthur that she'd been awake all night and was desperately trying to catch up on her sleep. Rosie had also met the big, grey cat. She'd narrowly escaped the cat's pounce and was then too frightened to sleep. "My heart was pounding," she said, smoothing her chest with her beak. Mouse knew exactly how she felt.

Rosie, who had first appeared quite angry, softened and before too long she was perched beside the boys. Arthur explained the game they were playing and she joined in, pecking at one of the scones.

Soon they were a trio to be admired. A mouse, a ladybird and a robin playing harmoniously together. Sadly, the trio were too busy having fun to notice the big, grey cat watching them from behind a nearby bench. The cat did not need to worry about owls in the daytime and was back to seek revenge. As Rosie pretended to brush scone crumbs from her red chest, the cat crept silently towards them, its body low to the ground.

Chapter 8. Cat Napped

The grey cat interrupted the picnic with an enormous leap and grabbed Mouse in its mouth.

"N o o o o !" shouted Arthur as the cat darted away with Mouse dangling from its jaw. Mouse tried to escape, but the cat's grip was too tight. He felt a sharp tooth dig into his side and it felt like his ribs were breaking. The cat jumped on to a fence and disappeared over it.

"We need to save him!" called Arthur to Rosie who was trembling from her beak to the tip of her tail.

"Too scared," she panted. She was torn between flying in the opposite direction, or helping to save her new friend.

"Well, I'll do it on my own then," said the brave little ladybird and he took flight, his good wing working at double speed. After only a few moments of hesitation, Rosie followed closely behind.

The park backed onto a row of houses and the grey cat had climbed over the fence into a back garden. It pranced proudly across the grass towards the back door of the house, looking extremely pleased with itself as it clutched its prize in its mouth. Mouse's body was hurting all over as the sharp tooth continued to poke into his ribs. Arthur and Rosie appeared over the fence and watched for a sign of life. Mouse looked very limp.

The cat vanished into the house through a small brown cat flap in the back door and Arthur, feeling relieved, spotted a flick of Mouse's tail. "He's still alive!" he cried.

On the other side of the door, the cat had stepped through the cat flap onto a tiled floor. It lowered Mouse onto the tiles and released him from its jaw.

"Ta da," said the cat in a cheery voice. Mouse opened one eye and peered up at the cat who appeared to be talking to someone else. Then as he looked around, Mouse's eyes met a terrifying image. His fur stood on end at the sight of a second big grey cat perched on the window sill.

Mouse wondered if his mind was playing tricks on him, if the pain from his broken ribs was causing him to hallucinate, but he realised quickly, as the second cat jumped down, that it was real. It slunk over to inspect Mouse and shoved its cold wet nose into Mouse's agonisingly painful ribs. Mouse winced. Both cats gave a sickening grin.

"Well done," said the second cat and it rubbed its cheek gently against the first in

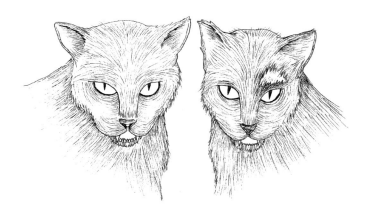

a display of affection. They were almost completely identical as they stood side by side, except for a white patch of fur above the second cat's left eye. Mouse considered the chances of him outwitting two cats; it was seriously doubtful.

Without warning, one of the cats gave Mouse a hard pat with its paw. Mouse rolled across the floor like a battered ball at which the cats both laughed out loud. They batted him back and forth, their cackles growing louder and louder and ringing in Mouse's bruised ears. Any glimpse of hope that Mouse might survive was rapidly fading with every whack.

One of the cats hit him with such force that he tumbled at speed into a cat basket in the corner of the room.

"GOAL!" it shouted and the wicked pair pranced around the room in celebration.

Mouse was relieved to feel the soft touch of the fluffy white blanket and prayed that the game was over. Then he prayed for a miracle. He thought of his grandpa and his mystery box. He didn't even care any more about vintage cheese or a special cheese knife; he just wanted to be away from this deadly duo.

The cats followed him over to the basket on tiptoes, their eyes wide with excitement. Mouse quivered. Suddenly, a voice called out from inside the house and broke the tension.

"Darcy, Charlie, where are you?" Mouse wondered if this was the miracle he'd been wishing for.

The cats' ears pricked up. "Mummy's brought you some tuna. Come on, girls." Mouse watched the cats closely and counted six long, anxious seconds before they finally reached a decision. They darted out of the room and into the hallway where two bowls of fresh fish were waiting, leaving Mouse alone.

Mouse took a deep breath and clambered to his feet, clutching his side. There was no time to waste. He was about to attempt to crawl out of the basket when he noticed a furry shape, half tucked beneath the blanket.

He shuffled towards it, sniffing the air,

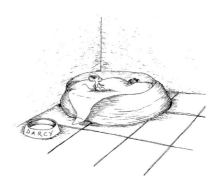

trying to work out what the shape was. There was a faint smell of cheese. When he was close enough to see clearly, he realised the shape was another mouse, curled-up, in a ball. The mouse was not moving at all.

Mouse reached out a paw and rubbed the mouse's fur gently, but no response.

"Hello," he whispered, but nothing. The cats must have killed the poor mouse and Mouse would surely be next! Mouse's gut churned with panic. He looked at the cat flap that he had just been dragged through and wondered if he would have enough strength to push it open from the inside.

He then looked back down at the curled-up, silent mouse and wondered where its family were and if he could let them know what had happened. He thought of his own parents and his grandmother and how devastated they would be to hear the news that Mouse had been killed by a cat. He felt an achy pang of sadness for this mouse's family.

KNOCK KNOCK!

Mouse jumped and looked to the door that the cats had just skidded out of. Luckily, they had not returned. Instead, to his astonishment, hovering at the window, were Arthur and Rosie! Arthur had the biggest grin on his face having spotted Mouse, still alive. He waved frantically and pointed to the cat flap below, encouraging Mouse to make a dash for it. Mouse then watched them courageously force open the cat flap and wedge it ajar with a couple of sticks.

"Come on!" shouted Rosie, peaking through the gap. Mouse wondered if the cats would be able to hear them from out in the hall, but he didn't have time to wonder as he heaved himself out of the basket on to the tiles.

"Wait," said a tiny voice. Mouse looked at the cat flap, but he didn't recognise the voice as Arthur's or Rosie's. He looked at the basket and saw the little ball of fur moving. Then a little mouse nose peeked out from beneath the blanket.

"Please help me," gasped the stranger.

Chapter 9. The Rescue Mission

Mouse could barely believe that the battered little mouse was alive! She had teeth marks on one ear, a deep scratch across her nose and bald patches where tufts of fur were missing.

Mouse looked at the poor state she was in and felt a surge of anger towards the cats who had hurt her. Mouse was determined to get her safely away.

"Don't worry," he said kindly, "You're safe now." The little mouse smiled then closed her eyes again, exhausted from their brief interaction.

Arthur and Rosie were watching on anxiously, aware that at any moment now the cats would be finishing their fish and would be back for dessert. Arthur called through the cat flap to hurry Mouse along.

Mouse grabbed the little mouse and heaved her on to the floor. He dragged her over to the cat flap, trying to be quick, but gentle. Mouse guessed that one of her legs might be broken as it dangled lifelessly. Mouse lifted her out of the cat flap and was greeted by Arthur with an enormous hug. Mouse wondered if he would ever let go.

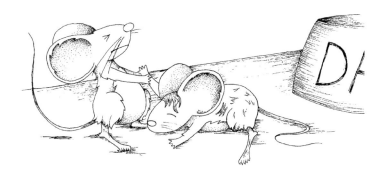

"Quick, she's very weak. We need to get her away," panted Mouse and he headed for the long grass. She stirred slightly as he carried her, but not for long.

Mouse hobbled across the patio and had just reached the lawn when he heard angry meows from inside the house.

"You go," said Rosie, "I've got this," and she waved goodbye to Mouse and Arthur. She was no longer shaking and had been inspired by Mouse and Arthur's incredible bravery. She perched on the handle of a full watering can that stood beside the back door and waited.

A second later, both cats came crashing out of the cat flap. One of the cats spotted the robin and leapt, but she was too quick. She shot upwards and did a backwards somersault. The cat collided with the watering can and sent it flying, covering itself from head to tail in freezing water. It squealed and dashed back inside, closely followed by its cowardly companion.

Mouse and Arthur had safely reached the fence at the back of the garden thanks to Rosie. They squeezed through a gap in the panels and searched as quickly as they could for somewhere to hide. Mouse spotted a small hole in the ground that was just big enough for them all. He swiftly checked that the hole was not already occupied. Luckily, it was vacant and he led them inside.

The hole was dark and damp, but safe. They waited in the darkness in silence before regaining the energy to speak. Mouse licked his cuts and bruises while Arthur stroked the little mouse's head as she rested.

"Wait here," said Mouse at last breaking the quiet. "I'll be back; don't follow me." Arthur went to protest, but thought better of it. Mouse's determined expression was back with a vengeance.

Mouse wriggled out of the hole and limped across the tree roots. He'd left his backpack at their picnic spot and it contained his precious letter from his grandfather. He searched the grass where they'd been pretending to picnic and found his bag exactly where he'd left it. It was almost too good to be true, or perhaps luck was just finally on his side.

He searched the ground for food to give to the injured mouse. He sniffed at the grass, but he wasn't exactly sure what he was sniffing for. There were no scents of croissants, tarts or pastries.

He was close to giving up when a sweet smell flooded his nostrils. He followed his nose to a pile of chestnuts in their spiky cases. Some of the cases had little splits on the sides. Mouse carefully peeled one open and nibbled the chestnut inside. It was delightful! He scooped up as many as he could carry and dragged a large leaf, still full of last night's raindrops, back to the hole. He wondered how he was even able to walk let alone carry his hoard. Adrenaline seemed to be keeping him going.

Spurred on by the fact he was still alive, Mouse continued to think quickly. His grandfather would have been proud. Once he'd reached their hiding place, he emptied the contents of his bag, pulled the thread stitching from the seam and used it to bind the little mouse's broken leg to his toothbrush like a splint. She flinched as Mouse straightened her leg and strapped it into position. He slid one of his slippers beneath her head like a pillow and encouraged her to eat and drink.

It appeared to be helping and she was already looking a little brighter. She asked Mouse to come closer and he willingly obliged and leaned forward. She placed an unexpected gentle kiss on his fluffy cheek.

Chapter 10. Lavender

With the touch of her soft lips, Mouse's cheeks turned bright red and his stomach did a somersault. Luckily, the little mouse didn't appear to notice his scarlet cheeks in the partial darkness and she closed her eyes again to rest. Mouse and Arthur guarded the entrance to the hole while she slept.

"I can see in the dark," whispered Arthur in Mouse's ear. Mouse blushed again. "I'm a bit insulted I didn't get a kiss," he joked. He teased Mouse and asked if he was in love, thinking of the list of tasks.

"Don't be ridiculous," Mouse replied stubbornly. "I don't even know her name."

That wasn't an issue for long for when the little mouse next woke, she felt well enough to sit up and chat. Her name was Lavender and it suited her perfectly. She was kind and funny and pretty. They talked and giggled, like they had with the robin. Mouse wondered what had happened to Rosie and he made a promise to himself that once Lavender was safe, he would return to thank Rosie properly.

They decided to spend the rest of the day and night in the hole. Mouse relished the opportunity to learn all about Lavender. She told Mouse that she had always lived outdoors and called herself a street-mouse. At first Mouse felt sorry for her for not having a proper home. But when she spoke of all the wondrous things she'd seen and done, he was almost jealous. She told him all about her travels across the country, hopping on trains and buses, visiting different towns and cities. She had incredible stories of the countryside with its rolling hills and fresh green grass, then amazing tales of cities with enormous buildings and countless cafés and restaurants.

"But don't you get lonely?" Mouse asked, thinking of his parents and his grandparents and how they'd always been by his side.

"Of course not!" she replied. "I make a new friend every day!" Mouse liked the idea of making friends. He already had three new friends and he'd not been away from home for very long at all. He imagined all the friends he would have by now, if he had been born a street-mouse.

Lavender's stories were endless. Mouse kept asking for more and more, his eyes wide with anticipation. When she grew tired of storytelling, Mouse shared his own. He told Lavender about the mystery box and how this was the very first time he'd been out of his mouse hole. Mouse recited his grandfather's list; "Drink rain water from a puddle, make a new friend, outwit a cat."

"And an owl!" interrupted Arthur eagerly.

Mouse grinned and then continued. "Have a picnic in the park, try the Brie cheese in Pierre's and ride a bus." He shot a look at Arthur and begged with his eyes for him not to mention number 7. He did not want Lavender to know that the final task was to fall in love.

"Hooray, you've done them all!" said Arthur with a cheer, to Mouse's great relief. Mouse was surprised that he wasn't leaping for joy himself; his enthusiasm had almost completely gone. Hearing Lavender's incredible stories had made his tasks sound so easy and trivial. Lavender must have travelled on the bus a hundred times and she said she was always making new friends.

Lavender was kind and hid any indication that she was not impressed. She was keen to know how Mouse had completed each task and had wonderful suggestions of what could possibly be inside the mystery box, none of which were food. She spoke of treasure maps, magic potions and secret family heirlooms. Mouse thought these sounded much more interesting than his own ideas and grew excited again; soon all the guessing would be over.

When the final glimpse of daylight faded, Mouse covered the entrance to the hole with leaves and twigs so that they couldn't be found and then he curled up next to Lavender and boldly made a reach for her paw. She happily accepted it.

Fall in love – check!

Chapter 11. Homeward Bound

The next morning they woke early and set out on their journey home. Mouse had invited Arthur and Lavender back to the bakery where his parents would be able to see to their injuries. Arthur and Mouse unravelled the napkin map and lay it flat on the grass, ready to plan their route.

"You don't need a map," laughed Lavender, "you've got me!" Mouse felt a lot safer with Lavender's street knowledge on their side, but he couldn't help but point out that she could barely stand. He wondered realistically how far he'd be able to carry her.

Mouse stopped wondering and sniffed. He could smell something particularly sweet close by, but not a nut this time. He followed the scent which led him to an old juice carton that had been tossed on the ground.

"Perfect!" he said, beaming, and he lifted Lavender onto it. He made sure the straw was securely attached to the carton then tucked the other end under his arm. Mouse heroically dragged the box like a stretcher across the grass towards the park entrance. Arthur cheered him on as if he was an athlete in a race. At first, this was a little annoying, but Mouse soon began to enjoy the whoops and calls.

"You can do it... it's not far now... mind the dog poo!"

Once they'd reached the park entrance, it took only seconds for Lavender to get her bearings.

"We'll be safer along the back roads," she said confidently, directing them away from the library and busy High Street. They travelled through deserted alleyways and quiet cobbled streets. Lavender knew exactly what to do if anyone came close to spotting them and she navigated their route with precision so that they approached the High Street from behind, avoiding the main road.

They peeked out from between the shops, with Mouse's bakery just two doors away. They waited until a little girl, who had just let go of her blue balloon, created the perfect diversion. Her mother tried to reach it, but it was too high and it quickly disappeared over the buildings. The girl screamed so loudly that her mother had to apologise to passers-by. The distraction allowed them to sneak unnoticed to the front door of the bakery.

Mouse didn't go straight in. He stopped to watch and listen to the buzz of the people on the busy street, trying to take it all in like a photograph. Soon he would be back in his mouse hole and all this would be a distant memory.

His stomach did a funny twisty turny thing. Mouse was relieved to see the bakery door; it meant safety and warmth and love. But it didn't mean excitement and it didn't mean friends. He wondered if his grandpa had struggled with the same decision all those years ago when he gave up his own adventurous life.

Mouse's adventures had been short, too short he thought.

For the moment, the one thing he was sure of was that Lavender needed taking care of and he knew the best place to do that would be in his family home. He hesitated no more and pulled the juice carton into the bakery. The door was ajar, unable to close as it was stuck on the corner of a rug that said WELCOME.

"Thank you," said Arthur to the rug. He helped lighten Mouse's mood. He always managed to see the fun side in everything.

Once safely inside, Mouse led them down twisting tunnels to his family home where his parents and grandmother were sitting quietly in the living room, twiddling their tails.

"Anyone home?" Mouse asked smiling and they all jumped to their feet. The four of them hugged for several minutes, his grandmother in floods of tears. Arthur cleared his throat, reminding Mouse that he wasn't alone. Mouse looked embarrassed, forgetting himself for a moment. He spoke very quickly, almost too quickly to follow, as he introduced Arthur to his family, explaining all about the cat, and, of course, Lavender, who was still clinging to the juice carton.

"Why don't we show Arthur your room?" suggested Mouse's father when he'd finished and he beckoned for Mouse and Arthur to follow him down the hallway. Mouse was a little surprised that he didn't have any questions or anything more to say about Mouse's great adventure. He got the impression that his father was trying to keep them away so that his mother and grandmother could see to the patient.

Mouse showed Arthur to his now rather plain looking bedroom. He'd never really noticed before how dim the colours were. No bright blue like the sky, or deep green like the trees. He remembered all of the colours and the wonderful smell of chestnuts warming in the sunshine. Arthur appeared politely impressed by Mouse's dull room.

Eventually Mouse and Arthur were invited back into the sitting room. Lavender's leg was now bandaged properly and she was almost unrecognisable. They had cleaned her wounds, combed her fur and tied a little pink bow around her neck.

"Wow," Mouse said out loud. She was absolutely beautiful!

Mouse spent the next few days always at Lavender's side. His parents made a bed for her in the corner of the living room and Arthur slept on a tuft of cotton wool beside Mouse's bed. Arthur didn't get much sleep; Mouse reminisced about their trip almost every night.

Once Lavender was showing signs of recovery, Mouse's grandmother reminded Mouse of his mystery box. She asked Mouse about his list of tasks and wanted every detail on how he had completed them. Mouse recounted the facts, while Arthur added the drama. He described the cat at least three times its actual size and kept referring to Mouse as "a true hero". The speed with which they'd shot along the gutter in a cardboard box was wildly exaggerated, but Mouse couldn't deny that it was quite a story. His parents and grandmother were filled with pride as they heard of Mouse's bravery and determination.

His grandma retrieved the box from a cupboard and handed it to Mouse with a smile. "You're ready."

Chapter 12. Inside The Box

Mouse carefully undid the latch on the side of the box and went to lift the lid. Arthur made an "ooohh" sound and clapped his hands like an excited drum roll. Mouse then heard him quietly wish for strawberry jam.

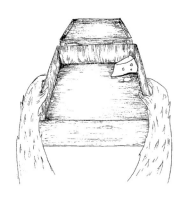

Mouse opened the box and to his surprise, found a very small piece of cheese. It looked rather insignificant in the corner of the wooden box. Mouse took a big sniff and scrunched up his nose; it was cheddar, his least favourite cheese. Mouse wondered why his grandfather had left him such an uninspiring chunk of cheddar.

"Try it then," prompted Mouse's grandma with a smile. Perhaps it tasted better than it looked, thought Mouse, and he forced a hopeful smile back. Then he broke the cheese into smaller pieces with his claws so that it could be shared between his family and friends. His parents were proud to see their once food obsessed son generously sharing the food between them.

As he broke the chunk of cheese apart, Mouse's paw hit something hard. He brushed the crumbles away and found a tiny brass key. His heart did a little leap and he let out an excited squeak. The cheese was not the gift after all; that was just to throw Mouse off the scent, literally!

The others, who were all watching Mouse intently, breathed a silent sigh of relief; everyone was quite glad that they didn't have to eat any.

Mouse admired the delicately ornate key until his grandmother pulled an envelope from a pocket in her pinafore and handed it to him. He beamed at the sight of his grandpa's wiggly writing on the front.

The envelope felt stuffed full in his paws. He carefully opened it, as wads of paper and napkins tried to burst out. The most obvious piece of parchment at the front appeared to be a letter. Mouse unfolded it, took a deep breath and read...

To my dearest Grandson,

The fact you are reading this letter means that you must have completed my list of tasks. Hooray, well done, Mouse! I am so proud of you; I never doubted you for a second. I hope it was as exciting and eventful as I dreamed it would be for you. If it was, you will, I'm sure, be desperate to get back out to the big wide world. I really hope that cheese and pastries are no longer the most important things in your life. I'm sorry for tricking you with the awful cheddar... I couldn't resist, and I wasn't going to waste a precious slice of Brie!

This little key will unlock a beautiful mouse hole, yours to call your own. I built it a long time ago when I was travelling, but your grandmother stole my heart and I followed her here to London. I do not regret that decision for a second and we have had the most wonderful life in our homely bakery. The outside world is an incredible place, Mouse, but there will be a time when you are ready to stop and enjoy the quiet life, the family life. I knew that time had come the moment I met your grandma.

I had dreamed of taking you there myself one day, but the time was never quite right. I wanted to make sure that you would appreciate it and that you'd be brave enough and smart enough to survive the journey. I know now that you are ready. You see... the mouse hole is in France, right in the heart of Paris, with spectacular views overlooking the Eiffel Tower!

Paris is home to some of the best cheeses in the world and the most beautiful sights you'll ever see.

Live your life to the fullest, Mouse, and enjoy the journey. I will be with you every step of the way. Remember, adventure is the most precious gift and must be treasured.

All my love, Grandpa."

Mouse finished reading the letter, tears streaming down his cheeks and those of everyone listening. He tried to swallow the lump in his throat and scanned the rest of the envelope's contents. It was stuffed with maps, pages from guide books, restaurant menus, notes and much more.

His grandfather's curly writing was everywhere offering quips, top tips, recommendations and more tasks.

Must see views from the top of the Eiffel Tower -
DO NOT CLIMB ON A WINDY DAY

Try the macaroons at Cafe Monsieur Benjamin -
THEY ARE EXQUISITE

Beware of the metro rats -
THEY ARE ENORMOUS AND NOT VERY FRIENDLY

Drink from the fountains in Luxembourg
Gardens -
WATCH OUT FOR THE PIGEONS

Visit Sacre Coeur -
EVEN MORE SPECTACULAR AT NIGHT

"Well?" asked Mouse's grandmother with anticipation. Mouse did not need to consider his answer. He felt completely and utterly

sure that this quest would be his best yet! He didn't need to say yes, his expression confirmed it. Lavender threw her arms around Mouse's neck and kissed his cheek again. This time everyone saw him blush. "I've always dreamed of going to Paris!" she cried.

With the help of his grandmother's knowledge and his parents' unconditional support, Mouse, Lavender and Arthur started planning straight away, mapping their journey across London and on to Paris. Mouse's grandfather had left him details of the Eurostar, an enormous train that travelled under the sea all the way to France. Mouse was a little disappointed that they weren't actually travelling by star.

Before they could depart, Mouse had one last job to do. He tracked Rosie down and thanked her for helping them to escape the big grey cats. Much to everyone's delight, their trio of explorers become four. The plucky little robin could not resist the promise of adventure and was the perfect addition to their funny little crew!

Live life to the full – check!